HOW TO GROW

HAPPINESS

A JEROME THE GNOME ADVENTURE

For Laurel and Josh, wishing you
a lifetime of happiness together.
—K.D.

For Emily, James, David, and Daniel.
—M.K.

ISBN 978-1-338-55762-6

Text copyright © 2018 by Kelly DiPucchio. Illustrations copyright © 2018 by Rodale Inc. All rights reserved.
Published by Scholastic Inc., 557 Broadway, New York, NY 10012, by arrangement with Random House Children's Books,
a division of Penguin Random House LLC. SCHOLASTIC and associated logos are trademarks
and/or registered trademarks of Scholastic Inc.

The publisher does not have any control over and does not assume any responsibility for author
or third-party websites or their content.

12 11 10 9 8 7 6 5 4 3 2 1   19 20 21 22 23 24

Printed in the U.S.A.   40

First Scholastic printing, April 2019

Design by Eric Wight and Jeff Shake

HOW TO GROW HAPPINESS

A JEROME THE GNOME ADVENTURE

KELLY DiPUCCHIO

PICTURES BY **MATT KAUFENBERG**

SCHOLASTIC INC.

W arble flew through the Garden of Wonder into Jerome's open window. "I brought you something special today," she chirped.

Jerome examined the tiny black seed resting on the window ledge.

"What kind of seed is that?" asked the curious inventor.

Warble smiled proudly. "It's a seed of happiness!" she declared.

Jerome, being a collector of treasures and trinkets, was very interested.

He reached for a glass jar on the shelf and emptied the contents into his hand.

"I will trade you this bit of red yarn for that seed," he said to his small friend.

Warble looked pleased. "That yarn will be perfect for my spring nest," she sang. "Thank you!" She scooped up her …d flew away.

Jerome dropped the seed into his empty jar.
He sat at his table waiting to feel happy.

When nothing happened, he tapped
impatiently on the glass.

TING!
TING!
TING!

Still nothing.

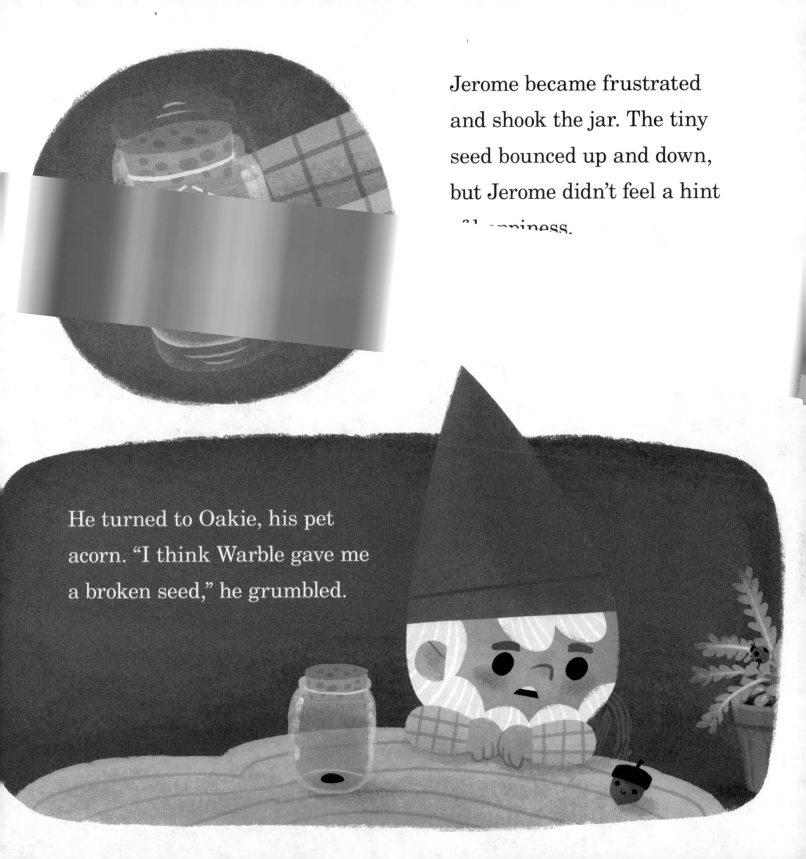

Jerome became frustrated and shook the jar. The tiny seed bounced up and down, but Jerome didn't feel a hint of happiness.

He turned to Oakie, his pet acorn. "I think Warble gave me a broken seed," he grumbled.

"A broken seed? Where?" asked Nutilda as she burst through the front door. Beamer, the robot, followed close behind.

Jerome showed his jar with the seed inside to his friends.
"...not broken," insisted Beamer. He pointed to his
...ds a little sun to work. Like me!"

Jerome agreed. He took his jar outside,
placed the seed on a rock in the hot sun,
and counted to 10. He sighed loudly.
"I'm still not feeling happy."

Sir Surly. "You

ed

"Of course," Jerome said to the turtle. "Why didn't I think of that?"

He tossed the seed into the pond.

"Good heavens!" cried Sherwin Wigglesworth, inching
his way toward the shore. "Not that much water!"

The worm climbed up on the rock. "I know a thing or two about gardening!" he boasted. "Your seed needs dirt. But not just any dirt—dirt with egg shells, coffee grounds, and banana peels."

Jerome smirked. "Who knew a little seed could eat so much?"
He fished the seed out of the pond, then covered it with dirt
and his morning trash.

Aroma joined the circle of friends. "What is everyone looking at?" she asked.

"Warble gave Jerome a broken seed of happiness and we're trying to fix it," Nutilda explained to the skunk.

"We've tried sun,"
said Beamer.

"And water," said Sir Surly.

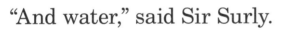

"And dirt," said Sherwin.

"But I still don't feel very happy," Jerome complained.
"As a matter of fact, I'm feeling angry with Warble for
taking my red yarn and giving me a worthless seed."

"...dear," whimpered Aroma, accidently spraying her scent.
...for unpleasant situations.

They made her nervous.

Glinda, the butterfly fairy, fluttered over to the troubled group. "You all forgot something important!" she chimed in.

"What's that?" asked Jerome, feeling more discouraged than ever.

"Love! The best things always grow from love," she said, disappearing over the bramble bush.

Jerome thought about what Glinda said. He suddenly felt compassion for the tiny, helpless seed, who must be feeling lonely buried beneath the heap of dirt and trash.

". . . . . . k " he told his friends.

Jerome returned with a jar filled with his favorite stones.

He placed the stones around his makeshift garden.

teensy bit happy.

Jerome tended to his seed every day,
making sure it got just the right
amount of sun,

water,

food,

and love.

He watched a short green sprout
grow into a long green vine.

As the vine grew,

happiness grew and

grew

until one day . . .

"FRIENDS!"

Jerome called out cheerfully.

"Come quickly!"

Jerome's friends gathered around him.

"Look!" he exclaimed, pointing to his garden.

The tiny black seed had grown into

...termelons!

"I'm sorry I ever doubted you,"
Jerome apologized to Warble.

"It's okay," said the bird. "Sometimes growing happiness
takes a little hard work and patience."

"And sun!"

"And water!"

"And dirt!"

"And love!
Don't forget the love!"

The friends laughed and enjoyed a summer picnic in the Garden of Wonder. They each went home that day with their own seeds of happiness.

KELLY DiPUCCHIO

is the *New York Times* best-selling author of over twenty-five books for children including *Grace for President*, *Gaston*, and *Everyone Loves Cupcake*. Kelly's happy place is at home in Michigan with her family and three dogs.

MATT KAUFENBERG

is a freelance illustrator who has worked for Playskool, Nick Jr., Facebook, and more. He lives in Minnesota with his wife and their four kids. *How to Grow Happiness* is his first picture book.